THIS BLOOMSBURY BOOK

BELONGS TO

....

For Granny, with love

First published in Great Britain in 2001 by Bloomsbury Publishing Plc
38 Soho Square, London, W1D 3HB
This paperback edition first published in 2002

Copyright © Dawn Apperley 2001
The moral right of the author/illustrator has been asserted

A CIP catalogue record of this book is available from the British Library
ISBN 0 7475 5543 5

Designed by Dawn Apperley

Printed in Hong Kong by South China Printing Co.

5 7 9 10 8 6 4

Don't Wake the Baby!

Dawn Apperley

BLOOMSBURY
CHILDREN'S
BOOKS

Baby is sleeping.
Lily-Lu is playing,
just quietly building a tower
higher and higher.
'1, 2, 3,' counts Lily-Lu.

When ...

Shhhhh, Lily-Lu, don't wake Baby!

Baby is sleeping.
Lily-Lu is tiptoeing,
creeping and crawling,
quietly rustling,
looking for bugs —
being very, very quiet.

When ...

... uh oh!

whoosh!

Shhhhh, Lily-Lu, don't wake Baby!

Baby is sleeping.
Lily-Lu is busy.
Busy buzzing.
'I am a very, very quiet bee,' hums Lily-Lu,
'zzzzzzzzz.'

When ...

Wheeeeee!

Shhhhh, Lily-Lu, don't wake Baby!

Baby is sleeping.
Lily-Lu is frog hopping.
'Hop, hop, hop,' sings Lily-Lu.
Big hop, little hop, big hop across the stream.

When ...

... uh oh!

Splash!

Shhhhh, Lily-Lu, don't wake Baby!

Baby is sleeping.
Lily-Lu is dancing,
skipping, leaping, whirling and twirling —
doing acrobats.

When ...

Shhhhh, Lily-Lu, don't wake Baby!

Baby and Lily-Lu are sleeping.
Both are dreaming.
No noise now.
No sound at all.
All is very quiet.

When ...

Wahhhhh!

Baby is wide awake! Crying and screaming —
being very, very noisy!
Shhhhh, Baby, don't wake Lily-Lu!

Enjoy more great picture books from Bloomsbury ...

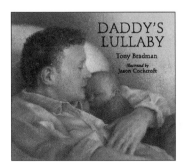

Daddy's Lullaby
Tony Bradman &
Jason Cockcroft

Five Little Fiends
Sarah Dyer

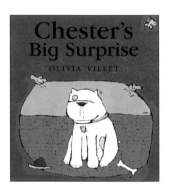

Chester's Big Surprise
Olivia Villet